BUSH STATION BOYS

Written by **Judy Langley**

Illustrated by **Wendy Kikugawa**

New Hope
Birmingham, Alabama

New Hope
P.O. Box 12065
Birmingham, AL 35202-2065

Dewey Decimal Classification: CE
Subject Headings: AFRICA—JUVENILE LITERATURE
                                        MISSIONARY KIDS
                                        MISSIONARY STORIES
Series: Land Far Away
ISBN: 1-56309-219-0
N978107•0597•5M1

Dedication

To the missionaries and MKs of Zimbabwe and Togo.

To missionary heroes serving God all over the world.

To future missionaries reading
"Land Far Away" right now.

Where I grew up
In a land far away,
My missionary family
Cared for people each day.

Our hospital and schools,
And the church in our town,
Were the heart of the bushlands*
For villages around.

*The bushlands is a large, sparsely settled area,
usually covered with small bushes.

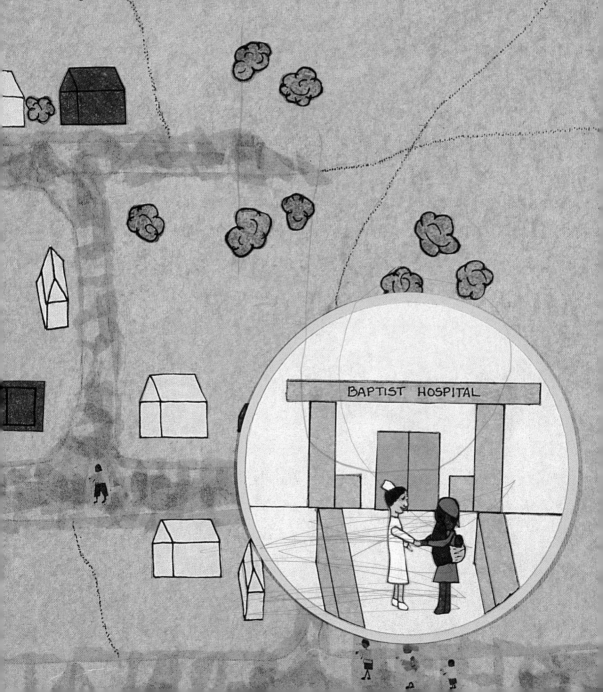

Our airplane brought patients
Who lived miles away,
And our doctors and nurses
Worked hard night and day.

They told stories of Jesus,
His love and His grace,
As they cared for sick people
In this loving place.

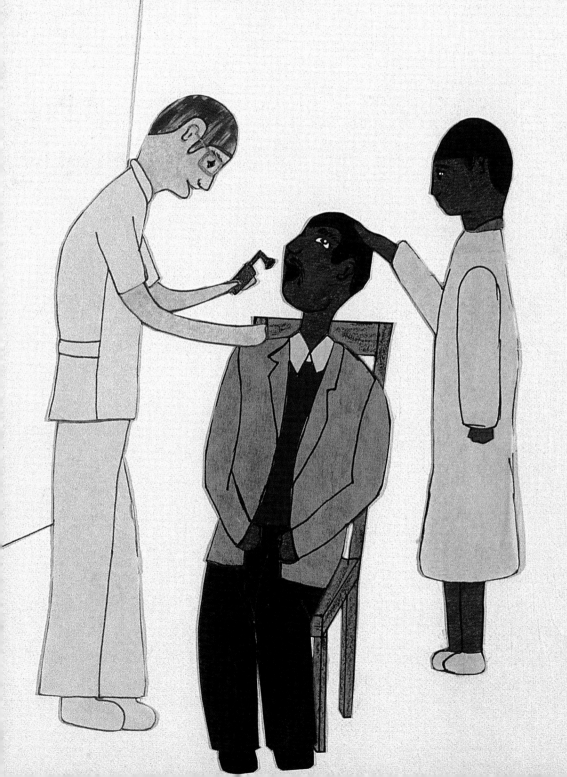

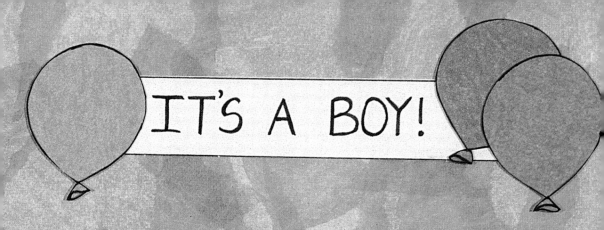

The hospital was special
To my family and me,
'Cause my brother was born there
When I was just three.

I helped Mom to feed him
And bathe him so clean.
Then, we'd put him to bed
'Neath a 'mosquito-net' screen.

And early each morning
Before the cool would pass,
We awoke to beautiful singing;
Students preparing for class.

The students who boarded
Lived just 'cross the street.
And getting to know them
Was part of my week.

Missionary teachers
Worked hard every day
Teaching their students
To follow God's way.

Running the mission
Was a very big task.
And it took lots of planning
To make supplies last.

So our lorry** would travel
To town for supplies
For groceries and letters
And often a surprise!

**A lorry is a large truck.

At the toot of the horn,
We'd rush down to greet
Our friends and our neighbors
As we met in the street.

Holidays were special,
We'd feast and we'd play,
Or go to the river,
In the cool of the day.

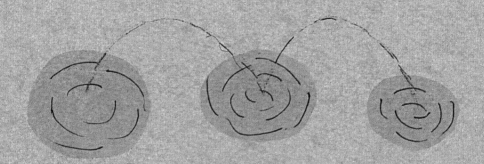

We'd cook out and skip rocks,
And have so much fun,
And we'd sing 'round our campfire
Of Jesus, God's Son.

My missionary family
Helped teach me, you see.
They were part of my life
And heroes to me.

Yes, I grew up in a land far away,
With people who loved me
And showed me God's way.

SUGGESTED ACTIVITIES

Increase children's awareness of other cultures by participating in the following activities.

Tell me a story, please!

Our missionary kids (MKs) liked to play a game with their aunts and uncles (MKs often call other missionaries their aunts and uncles since they are like family members). Each MK would take turns asking missionaries, "Please, tell me a story about _____ ." (Fill in the blank with names of animals, people, objects, or situations.) The missionary would tell a story from his or her own life experiences while trying to reinforce Christian values and Christian character traits. Play this game with your family at a picnic and/or a church event.

Or, be a storyteller! Explain to your child that because many African families do not have a television, listening to a storyteller is often a favorite pastime of many African children. Ask your child if he or she would like to be a storyteller. Then allow your child to tell you a story; it may be fiction or non-fiction. After the child finishes his or her story, ask the child to listen as you tell a story. You may tell a story about your childhood, a fictional character, or about Bible characters.

Yellow Rice

2 cups instant rice
2 cups water
1/2 cup brown sugar
1 teaspoon salt
1/2 cup seedless raisins
1 1/2 teaspoon turmeric
1 tablespoon margarine

Add all the ingredients except the rice to the water. Bring the mixture to a boil. add the rice. Remove the ric mixture from the heat. Cover. Let the mixture stand for 5 minutes.

ABOUT THE AUTHOR

From 1971 until 1983, Judy Langley and her husband, Phil, served as missionaries in Zimbabwe and Togo. Their sons Anthony and Jonathan, who both grew up in Africa, provided the inspiration for the narrations in the "Land Far Away" series. Since leaving Africa, Judy and Phil have traveled extensively doing a variety of missions work in Colorado, New Mexico, and Hawaii. Appointed by the North American Mission Board, they currently live in Fresno, California, where Phil serves as the Director of the Department of New Church Extension for the California Southern Baptist Convention.

ABOUT THE ILLUSTRATOR

Wendy Kikugawa was born and raised in Hawaii. She enjoys reading, drawing, baking, cooking, and doing all kinds of crafts. Wendy continues to be amazed at how God works in her life, and she is especially grateful for the opportunity to illustrate the "Land Far Away" series.

If you enjoyed Bush Station Boys,
be sure not to miss The Elephant Path,
Clay Homes, Bushland Backyard, and
Down African Roads, Books One, Two,
Three, and Four in the Land Far Away series.
Look for these titles in your local Christian
bookstore, or order them by calling
1-800-968-7301.